Queen Mariella
and the Fable of the Peony

Written by
James P. Menconi

Illustrated by
Michelle Marie Menconi

Copyright © 2025 **Donquijote Publishing**

All rights reserved. No part of this publication may be reproduced, distributed, or transmitted in any form or by any means, including photocopying, recording, or other electronic or mechanical methods, without the prior written permission of the publisher, except in the case of brief quotations embodied in critical reviews and certain other noncommercial uses permitted by copyright law. For permission requests, write to the publisher, addressed "Attention: Book Rights and Permission," at the address below.

Published in the United States of America

ISBN 979-8-89395-810-2 (SC)
ISBN 979-8-89395-809-6 (Ebook)

Library of Congress Control Number: 2024921818

Donquijote Publishing
145 W Broadway
Long Beach, CA 90802, USA
jamesmenconi@yahoo.com

Order Information and Rights Permission:

Quantity sales. Special discounts might be available on quantity purchases by corporations, associations, and others. For details, contact the publisher at the address above.

For Book Rights Adaptation and other Rights Permission. Call us at toll-free 1-888-945-8513 or send us an email at admin@stellarliterary.com.

Note to teachers, parents, gardeners, and most importantly smart kids everywhere:

The story of "Queen Mariella and the Fable of the Peony" is a fictionalized tale of how the ants help peonies blossom to be one of the prettiest and fullest flowers in the garden to herald the coming of spring. It will help children learn about the different flowers in the garden and how insects such as the ants help them. Another goal of this book is to help children develop character education skills, and help them understand how important it is to understand a nurturing love or respect for one another and be courageous enough to stand up for it. Spanish words are used to introduce readers to a bicultural and bilingual world and to learn to appreciate diversity. I hope children and adults of all ages will enjoy this fanciful tale that relates to the real world in many ways, and share it with their friends for generations to come.

Dedication

This book is dedicated to my mother, Marie Ella Mosebach Menconi;

my daughter, Lynnette Cecelia Menconi;

my granddaughters, Mia and Jenna;

and to Gail Arnold's 4th/5th Grade Young Authors,

at Monroe School in Chicago, who

shared a love of writing with me.

Acknowledgments

To Richard Cozza for his astute editing and advice, and Michelle Menconi for her beautiful illustrations.

Language Key

Abuelito
grandpa

¡Venga aqui en mi jardin!
Come here in my garden!

¿Que tienes?
What do you have?

mi hijo
my son

jitomates
tomatoes

tu favorito
your favorite

muy misterioso
so mysterious

Y, mi hijo
Well, my son....

¡No te preocupes, mi hijo!
Don't worry, my son!

¿Que es lo próximo a pasar?
What happened next?

¡Abuelito, no me digas!
Grandpa, don't tell me!

Que maravilloso
How marvelous

Queen Mariella and the Fable of the Peony

"¡Abuelito! ¡Abuelito!"

"¡Diego! ¡Diego, venga aqui en mi jardin! Look what I have to show you here in my garden!"

"¡Abuelito! ¡Abuelito! What do you have?" "¿Que tienes?"

"Look, I'm planting these beautiful flowers in my garden!"

"What kind of flowers are they Grandpa?"

"I have some rose bushes that will have a magical fragrance in the summer. They'll keep those bees busy all summer long. Then for the spring, I'm planting these pretty pansies that will take on the faces of children. Diego, do you see your face on them?"

"Oh, Grandpa! I do. I do! What other kinds of flowers are you planting in your magical garden, Abuelito?"

"Well, I'm planting some beautiful sunflowers. They will bring in the songbirds all summer and even into the fall, so my garden will be a mystical place to think about the blessings of life. Then in the back, I'll plant some hollyhocks that will grow to be taller than you, mi hijo, so they can keep an eye on you wherever you may go."

"Oh Grandpa, it's as if your garden is watching over me."

"Well, then you'll always know that when you come into my garden you'll always be reminded of me."

"Abuelito, you talk as if your garden is alive?"

"Si, mi hijo. It's alive with adventure and excitement day in, day out. It's filled with the mysteries of life. It's also filled with the songs of life made by the beautiful songbirds that come to visit, the humming of the hummingbirds, and the bees that come to make the food of life, honey and pollen. The garden is filled with the laborers of life. For the farmers of life are the ants and the ground worms that till the soil and make it so rich; rich enough that we can grow beautiful flowers and strong crops like corn, spinach and my tasty tomatoes or jitomates."

"Grandpa, which flower is your favorite, tu favorito? Which one is the most beautiful?"

"Y mi hijo…. It's the peony. It's the beautiful pink flower that's right over there. Don't you see it; so beautiful, so colorful, so full of lush magical petals that fragrance the air in the spring and tell of the coming of spring. It's a regal flower that's bowing down to its creator who made it so beautiful, fragrant, and lush."

"¿Abuelito, Abuelito, why is the peony so magical, so mystical, muy misterioso?" "Y, mi hijo, it's bowing down so it can give thanks to the tiny creatures that give it the magical beauty it possesses."

"Grandpa, who are these tiny creatures? "Ants, mi hijo!"

"Ants, Grandpa? Why is the peony bowing down to the ants?"

"Well, in a time long, long ago, there was a most beautiful garden, much more beautiful than the one I have. It was a garden full of flowers, fragrant, and bright. It was a garden full of life and harmony. It was a garden that every one of God's creatures tiny and large enjoyed and cherished for its beauty and peacefulness. As the sun would rise, so would the flowers and the creatures of this most magnificent garden. The songs of the songbirds would awaken all the creatures to start their labors to make this garden the most special garden of all the beautiful gardens."

"Why was this garden so special, Grandpa?"

"Y mi hijo, in those days this garden was governed by Queen Mariella who was most adored and beloved by all the creatures of the garden. She was adored because she was so giving, loving, and thoughtful to all the creatures in her garden. It was a pure and natural love for each other. Whenever there was some creature in need, there was Queen Mariella, queen of the ants, to help them.

When the fox stubbed her toe with a thorn, Queen Mariella sent her worker ants to soothe the sore with a magical mud that comforted the fox so she could continue to feed her pups.

When the ladybug had trouble flying, Queen Mariella visited her and soothed her with a sweet-smelling potion made from the roses.

When the possum's paw got stuck in some kind of a trap, Queen Mariella sent her worker ants to gnaw away at the trap till the possum could escape.

When the baby rabbit lost his way, Queen Mariella sent her wisest ants to help him find his way home.

When her friend, Cousin Bee, had trouble with her stomach because she ate too much honey, Queen Mariella summoned her medicine drone to mix a special potion to put her friend at ease.

Because of all these deeds and her compassionate care of all the creatures in her garden, all the creatures in her garden shared a pure and natural love for each other and for Queen Mariella.

Now it came to be that one drone ant, by the name of Javier, had a special love for Queen Mariella. Javier was the bravest and most courageous of all the drone ants. He had a pure and natural love for her, not only because she was so considerate, kind, and beautiful, but because he had a most marvelous attraction to her. He was attracted to her true beauty. And it was said that Queen Mariella shared this attraction with Javier because he was so handsome, brave, and strong.

When they first saw each other, they looked into each other's eyes and saw a pure and natural love. It was this pure and natural love that drew them to each other. It was this pure and natural love that made them stand apart from the others. It was this pure and natural love that made their garden so harmonious and happy.

Javier knew it would soon be time to mate; for there is a time when all things small and large under the sun must share their love. This is our creator's great plan for all of us."

"Oh Abuelito, am I supposed to hear this part?"

"Why of course, mi hijo! This is what life is all about. Many in Queen Mariella's Garden knew that Queen Mariella's marriage to Javier would bless her garden for years to come. For their union would bless them with strong and healthy 'youngins', just like you, Diego. All the creatures in the garden gathered the most beautiful flowers and the most delicious foods in preparation for the most gala of all weddings. The garden had a hum to it as everyone became so merry in preparation for this most gala event. All the creatures loved Queen Mariella so much that they gave of their time willingly and freely.

The fox found some lovely twigs for the chamber room.

The possum found some lush leaves for their bed.

The bees brought their favorite clover honey for their wedding dinner.

The ladybugs brought the most fragrant and colorful flowers.

The baby rabbit found some choice carrots for the wedding meal.

Everything and everybody worked very hard to prepare for the most elegant of all marriages. Then....

One day before the wedding, Queen Mariella took ill with a strange illness. No one in the garden knew what caused it. It just happened. Several days before her marriage she became faint. She couldn't perform her normal duties and decided to go to her chamber room. All the doctor ants were summoned to her room to see what magic potion could be created to cure her. Everyone was perplexed and puzzled. They did not know what this disease could be. They tried all the potions they used in the past, but nothing seemed to help Queen Mariella. She was still sickly, not wanting to eat, or able to sleep. It was as if she was under some kind of mysterious spell.

They even sent word to the wise owl to see if he knew of a cure. No one seemed to know what to do. All the worker ants were sent out to the garden to see if a cure could be found. Father Possum knew of no cure. Ladybug knew of no cure. Father Fox knew of no cure. Mother Rabbit knew of no cure. They were all perplexed or confused. What should they do to keep Queen Mariella alive?

Javier was desperate. What should he do to save his pure and natural love? Then while he was in deep thought, he remembered that he had once heard the bees buzzing that there was a secret wax on a very special flower. When this secret wax melted down, it became a secret potion that helped one live a long and natural life. With this in mind, Javier scurried out to meet with Cousin Bee to find where this flower was located.

After a long journey, Javier met with Cousin Bee and told her of his problem. Cousin Bee became distressed upon hearing the news because she too had loved Queen Mariella. Cousin Bee remembered how compassionate Queen Mariella was in helping her get better after she was ill. She decided she would show Javier the location of this magical flower, a flower they had named the peony.

After a journey through the garden, Javier and Cousin Bee came upon a most beautiful corner of the garden that was filled with sunlight. It was as if the sun was helping them find their way to this mystical flower. As the sun shone brightly on the peony flower, its wax became soft and clear. Cousin Bee shouted to Javier, 'Go to the top of the bud and scrape off the wax. Then take the wax back to Queen Mariella to soothe her and cure her illness.'

Javier bravely climbed to the largest bud of the peony flower in the height of the sun's heat and scraped off the wax. It was an arduous task since the sun was so hot on this spring day, but he prevailed and made it to the top. He took as much wax as he could carry. As he scraped the wax, the most beautiful flower opened up and filled the garden with a most beautiful fragrance. Its fragrance was intoxicating and the beautiful pink colors of the peony flower lit up the garden as if there were pink clouds shining on a sunny day.

Upon returning to the colony, Javier sent all the soldier ants back to the peony patch to scrape all the wax necessary to have a cure for every ant that came down with the mysterious disease that made Queen Mariella sick. The soldier ants scurried toward the peony patch with fierce dedication to save Queen Mariella and any other infected ants in the colony.

Upon their journey back to the colony, Javier took the lead for his pure and natural love for Queen Mariella gave it urgency. As he and his soldier ants traveled through the garden, there stood their most hated predator, the wicked widow spider.

She stood there waiting in anticipation of the ants getting snared in her traps. For she and her fellow widow spiders laid traps of intricately woven webs throughout the garden since she had seen Javier and the other soldier ants go to the peony patch earlier in the day.

One by one, the soldier ants carrying their precious cargo of the wax potion were snared in the intricately woven webs. Desperately, they tried to escape since they knew how urgent it was to bring back their cargo. But it was to no avail since the webs were so perfectly designed. Soon there were only a few soldier ants left with Javier courageously in the lead.

Just as Javier and the surviving soldier ants made their way through the never-ending webs, there stood one last widow spider. It was the biggest widow spider they had ever seen. She stood there knowing that soon she was to have the finest meal of the day. Javier knew that this would be the battle of their lives, a battle like no other. A battle that would be written in history as the war of wars. So, Javier and his soldiers braced for what would indeed be the end of Queen Mariella's kingdom if they didn't triumph over the wicked widow spider.

Javier stirred his soldiers to triumph by retelling how compassionate and loving Queen Mariella was to all of them. If she died, her peaceful, beautiful, and natural kingdom in which all were so loving and caring would end. Javier's pure and natural love was so evident to all that they gathered every ounce of courage and charged the giant widow spider with all their ferocity even though they were few in numbers.

They battled, battled and battled. The wickedly woven webs caught many of the soldier ants and entangled them till their deaths. Many fought on with the greatest of persistence and strength. Leading the way was Javier for deep down in his soul he knew that there was no other pure and natural love like his love for Queen Mariella.

The battle was indeed fierce. Javier and the soldier ants fought their way through the webs and managed to attack the giant widow spider's clutches and claws time and time again. Many did not survive. Many were crumbled into little balls to lay in wait for the other widow spiders. Even Javier was badly injured with slashes from the spider's jaws."

"Abuelito, no me digas. Grandpa, don't tell me that Javier dies? What will happen to Queen Mariella's kingdom?"

"¡No te preocupes, mi hijo! Don't worry Diego. A pure and natural love will live on forever.

Javier garnered enough strength to battle on and on. Just when it looked as if he would fall to the clutches of the dreaded giant widow spider, Javier broke through the webs and the clutches of the spider to carry on in his journey. He knew that Queen Mariella and her kingdom had to survive and live on for the benefit of all the generations of ants in her colony. Queen Mariella's love had to be shared with many, many more. Queen Mariella's pure and natural love had to live on forever. Following him were the few soldier ants who too had survived the battle. Now he knew that he had just enough secret wax to save Queen Mariella."

"Oh, Abuelito! That was a tough battle, but what happened next? ¿Que es lo próximo a pasar?"

"Triumphantly, Javier and his soldier ants returned to the Queen Mariella's chambers. They were battered and bruised because they fought so valiantly. However, they were proud of themselves because now they had secured enough secret potent to save the queen. Holding back the pain, Javier gave the wax to the doctor ants that waited to care for the ailing queen.

Day after day, the doctor ants soothed the queen with the magical balm they made from the secret wax. Each day Javier waited in anticipation for his queen to be healthy once again. He remembered how their love filled the chamber with sweet music, sounds of joy, and happiness. He remembered how they romped through the clover fields in merriment. He remembered her kindness to all the creatures of their garden. He remembered her compassion for all those in need. Most of all he remembered how she filled him with a pure and natural love that made him tingle from antenna to antenna, an electrifying feeling.

The first day of treatment made no difference, Queen Mariella's health remained the same. However, with each passing day the sweet balm of the peonies' wax and the magical, mystical love that Javier had for her brought her back to health."

"¡Que maravilloso, Abuelito! How marvelous, Grandpa."

"Oh yes, que maravilloso! The only problem was that as Queen Mariella's health got better, Javier's health and strength slowly weakened. He had fought so valiantly to save the queen that he had no strength left. For him, his own health wasn't of importance. He knew that saving the queen and bringing her back to health so that her kingdom would live on was the only thing of importance. So, when he heard Queen Mariella's happy, healthy voice saying, 'I love you Javier!', he breathed his last breath. He had saved her pure and natural love to treasure in his heart. He had saved Queen Mariella's kingdom in which all the creatures small and large lived-in harmony and love; a pure and natural love that Queen Mariella gave to them."

"I love you, Javier!"

"Abuelito, that can't be the end of the story!"

"No, no, Diego. Queen Mariella lived on to lead a most marvelous life for she too treasured that pure and natural love she had for Javier, and that Javier had for her. It was a love so strong that nothing could kill her, and her love for Javier would only be rivaled by the love she had for all the creatures of her kingdom. To celebrate this pure and natural love, each year Queen Mariella sends out all her soldier ants to gather as much secret peony wax from every peony patch throughout the world. It's a journey that heralds the coming of spring and life everlasting. It's a life that springs eternal with the hope for a pure and natural love like Queen Mariella's and Javier's. Then when the soldier ants eat off all the secret wax from the peony buds, a beautiful flower prettier and more fragrant than all the others in the garden is given to us to remind us of that pure and natural love. It's a hope eternal for better things to come."

"Abuelito, that's beautiful. You're the best! ¡Lo mejor!"

"No Diego. You're the best! ¡Lo mejor! What you need to remember is that we too are special, and we too can live in a kingdom as special as Queen Mariella's. A kingdom that is filled with a pure and natural love. Remember that when you come upon this pure and natural love, you need to stand up and be courageous and valiant just as Javier was. For when you come upon this pure and natural love, you need to treasure it in your heart so that it will live on forever and forever."

www.ingramcontent.com/pod-product-compliance
Lightning Source LLC
LaVergne TN
LVHW070536070526
838199LV00075B/6793